W9-BHN-726

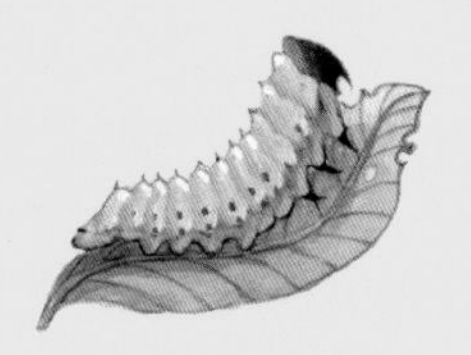

Hope Weavers

Brenda Ehrmantraut

Illustrated by Diana Magnuson

ISBN 978-0-9729833-8-9

Library of Congress Control Number 200903349

Designed by Doug Hagley
Printed in the United States of America

Printed by Bang Printing, Brainerd, MN, 2nd Ptg., 01/2010

Aberdeen, SD 57401

To order additional copies please go to:
www.bubblegumpress.net

Two little girls were having trouble sleeping.

Samira was scared. She curled into the tightest ball she could possibly make of herself in her bed of branches. She waited for tomorrow to come. She hoped it would be the day her family would reach the safe place.

Marisa was sad.
Tomorrow, her father
would be leaving.
He would be gone
a long time.

"Marco's sad, too,"
thought Marisa when
she heard her baby
brother cry. She
pushed the soft
comforter aside and
flopped out of bed.

She tiptoed to the door of her brother's room. In the dim light she watched her father lift the baby out of his crib and wrap him in a blanket. Father held the cocooned little boy in his strong arms and rocked him gently back to sleep.

Marisa turned to sneak back to her own bed, but the sight of her father's luggage stopped her. There were his bag and boots, his coat and helmet waiting by the front door. Her nose stung as tears formed.

She ran to her father. "I wish you didn't have to go," she sobbed. "Why do you, anyway?"

Father took a deep breath. “Of course I’d rather stay right here with you,” he assured her. He wiped her tears and tickled her cheek with a butterfly kiss.

“You know,” he said, “I think I might know someone who can explain why I have to go.”

“Who?” she asked curiously.”

“We’ll look for him tomorrow,” Dad promised.

The next morning they took a walk together. After a short time Dad announced, "Here he is!" and dropped a plump, fuzzy caterpillar into her hand.

Marisa gave her dad a questioning look. A bug was going to tell her why Dad was leaving?

"Caterpillars don't talk," she challenged.

"I think he has something to tell you if you are patient and watch him closely," Dad answered.

She shrugged, but agreed to keep the caterpillar. She decided to name him Chatterbox, since she expected him to talk to her.

Later that day Marisa watched the spot where her father's plane disappeared on the horizon. It trailed a stream of exhaust that would soon tie her world to a stranger's.

Samira and her family stopped walking long enough to share what little food they had left.

When an enormous plane flew overhead, Samira tried to reach the jetstream. "Maybe it's a rescue rope," she thought hopefully.

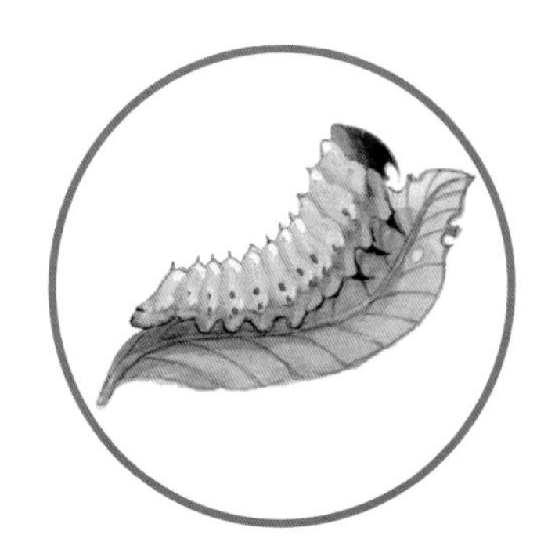

Marisa reported to Chatter, "Okay, Dad's gone. Now you can tell me why he went."

Chatter was busy eating. He didn't even look up.

"That's what I thought. You don't know either," she accused.

Samira and her family wearily approached the camp gate. The guards let them pass, then moved back into position.

Soldiers from many countries were posted around the camp for protection. In the glare of the sun, Samira thought it looked like a chain made of humans, linked arm in arm. A teardrop of relief ran down her cheek.

Samira's feet were blistered from the long walk. A soldier smiled at her and gently wrapped gauze bandages around them.

She relaxed as the white fabric that soothed her feet began to wrap her world in healing, too.

Mother showed Marisa a picture in the newspaper.

"Country Begins Recovery with Help," she read. The picture showed people in uniforms like Dad's. They were handing out bottles of water and taking care of people.

Marisa brought the newspaper picture to show Chatter. She spotted him hidden in the leaves. He was weaving back and forth, half-covered in a stringy looking coat.

"Now what are you doing?" she asked in surprise.

He was too busy to stop and talk. "I'll keep waiting," she sighed. "Like Dad said."

One day Marisa's teacher read a letter from the soldiers.

Dear Friends,

The children here have lost their homes and most of their clothing. They have no toys or school supplies. If you have any extra things you could share, please send them.

With love,

The Soldiers

Eagerly, the children hunted for things they could share. They wrapped their gifts with ribbons, and sent a special care package to the children.

Samira untied a red bow from her package. Inside she found pencils and a notepad. She held the precious supplies tightly and thought about returning to school.

Quietly, she collected the ribbons her friends had discarded. Like a rainbow after a storm, the ribbons brought a bright promise that things would one day return to normal.

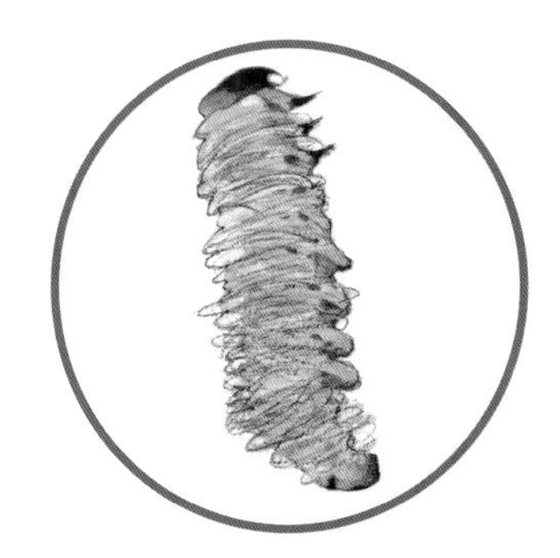

Before long, Marisa received an envelope in the mail. Inside was a colorful woven bracelet, a picture of a girl, and a note from her father.

Dear Marisa,

A new friend of mine made this for you. Samira is a refugee here at the camp. The refugees have been forced out of their homes and will live here in tents until it is safe to return. They were happy to get your package.

Love, Dad

Marisa wanted to show Chatter the bracelet and tell him about Samira, but all she found was a furry looking pod.

"Now how am I supposed to talk to you if you're playing hide and seek?" she scolded tenderly, knowing the worm was in there listening.

Once Samira's people felt secure in the cocoon of their camp, they began to join the soldiers in a daily rhythm.

Cooking pots bubbled with familiar smells.

Damaged roads were rebuilt.

Fishing boats rocked near the shore.

Cables stretched across the land.

Water gushed
from freshly
drilled wells.

Seeds sprouted
into promising
vines.

Needles mended
torn clothing.

Marisa received some good news. Dad would be returning home soon!

She went to tell Chatter, but found the cocoon was empty. Next to it was a delicate creature with wings. She looked at it in fascination. She knew it must be Chatter, but he looked so different. She wondered if he was finally ready to talk to her.

Samira had a surprise, too. She heard the rumble of trucks coming into camp. The whole place erupted in a flurry of activity as belongings were retrieved and tent stakes were pulled up. Everyone climbed aboard the trucks to return to their homes which were safe now.

The hardworking ropes and canvas that had given protection these long months now lay forgotten in limp piles.

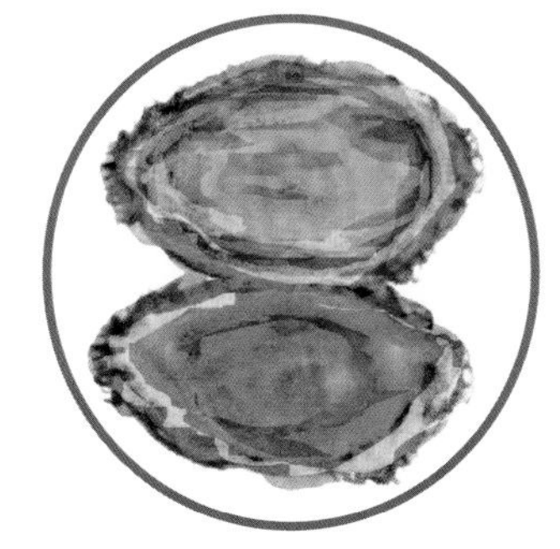

Marisa reached for the abandoned pod.

"Is this a magic hideout?" she asked the new Chatter.

Then her eyes widened in understanding.

"Oh! Is this what you came to tell me?" she asked excitedly. "Is Dad building a cocoon, too?"

Chatter seemed to fan his lovely wings in a "Yes."

Marisa smiled down at the silky pod in which Chatter had transformed.

Now she could imagine Samira in a cocoon, too. The layers of it were spun from healing bandages, nourishing steamy food, protective chains, rescue ropes, and mending threads.

And woven through it all were shiny ribbons of hope for the future.

Like Chatter, it was time for Samira to leave the cocoon and begin her bright, new life.

Two windows opened.
Two girls waved goodbye.

Both slept peacefully,
wrapped in hope.

Author's Note

Would you be surprised to hear that Chatter is not a butterfly? He is really a Luna moth. Caterpillars that become butterflies don't spin cocoons. They build a protective shell called a chrysalis. It is made from leaves and skin they have shed. A moth caterpillar can produce silk strands and spin a layer around the chrysalis to make a cocoon.

In this story, Chatter spins a cocoon and changes into a moth while a country heals from a disaster. In reality, it takes a long, long time for a country to recover from a natural disaster or war, sometimes many years. It takes some caterpillars only a few months to change from an egg to a moth or butterfly.

Dedication

For Mark, my cocoon and wings.

—B.E.

In honor of my nephews Bjorn, Jason, Nils and my niece, Solveig, for their military service in Iraq, Uzbekistan and Afghanistan, and my son Josh who served in Korea.

—D.M.

Special Thanks

To Tonya Sigl for asking for a book; Shirla Wells for insight and guidance; and everyone who has sacrificed their own family time to contribute to brighter futures for fellow humans.